Spot's Hospital Visit

Visit

Eric Hill

A Spot Storybook

Heinemann

"I'm ready!" Spot shouted to Tom
and Helen. They were going to see Steve,
who was in hospital with a
broken leg.

Tom had a ball for Steve, and Helen
was taking her doctor's bag and flowers.

"I have some fruit for Steve," said Spot, popping a grape into his mouth.

"We'd better hurry or there won't be any left!" Helen told him.

At the hospital, they found Steve's room and peeped in.

Steve waved. He was happy to see his friends.

"Thanks for coming," he called. "I love visitors, especially when they bring me presents!"

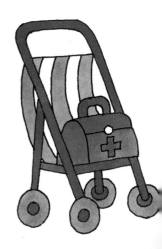

Spot was staring at the plaster cast on Steve's leg. "Doesn't that hurt?" he asked.

"Not at all," said Steve. "Anyway, it's coming off tomorrow."

"What? Your leg?" gasped Tom.

"No, silly. Just the cast."

"Who's been writing on your cast?"
asked Spot.

Steve laughed. "All my friends here.
The doctors and nurses and some of the
children too."

"I want to write my name," said Spot.
So he did, and then Tom drew
a funny face.

"What's this handle for?" Tom asked, as he started to turn it. Steve's head and shoulders rose into the air.

"Hey! Look at that!" shouted Tom.

Spot found another handle on the other side of the bed and began turning.

Steve's feet went up.

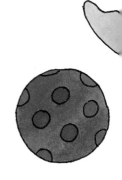

"Be careful!" Steve yelled. "You're not supposed to do that. I might break something else."

Suddenly the door opened and Nurse Rabbit came in with a wheelchair.

"Here, Steve," she said. "Why don't you take your friends to the playroom?"

"Look at all these toys," said Tom.
"I like this train," said Spot.
Helen went to her doctor's bag
and took out a green mask and gown.

"Let's play doctor," said Helen. So Tom sat down and Helen listened to his chest.

He began to laugh and twist around.

"Sit still!" Helen ordered. "You don't laugh and fool around when a real doctor examines you."

"But you're tickling me," giggled Tom.

"Let's pretend Spot has a broken leg," said Helen. She unrolled a bandage and wound it around Spot's leg.

"Put Spot in your pushchair, Helen!" shouted Steve.

"Tom, look at Spot," said Steve.
But Tom wasn't there.

Helen wheeled Spot into the hall and
Steve followed.

"Where can Tom be?"
he asked.

They looked in the X-ray room.

"This is the machine that took pictures of my leg," Steve told them.

"I know about X-ray machines," said Helen. "They're like cameras, but they take pictures of your bones."

"I don't see Tom in here," said Steve. "Do you?"

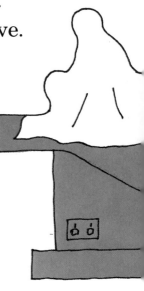

As the three friends turned around
to leave, a loud voice shouted, "BOO!"
They all jumped.

There sat Tom. He'd been hiding
under a sheet all the time.

"Did I scare you?" he laughed.

Visiting time was over, so they said good-bye to Steve and went to Spot's house. Sally was at the door.

"Spot!" she cried. "What happened to your leg?"

"Don't worry," Spot told her. "Helen was just playing doctor."

"I liked the hospital," said Spot.
"We had fun. I think I'd like to be
a doctor when I grow up."

"Maybe you will," said Sally.
"But in the meantime, Steve will soon be
out of the hospital, and you can all play
doctor at home."

"Great!" said Spot.